THIS WALKER BOOK BELONGS TO:

_____

_____

_____

_____

For my mother and father

I would like to thank
Helen Read for the decorative borders
she designed and painted
so beautifully.

F.M.

First published 1992 by
Walker Books Ltd
87 Vauxhall Walk
London SE11 5HJ

This edition published 1994

4 6 8 10 9 7 5 3

Text © 1992 Walker Books
Illustrations © 1992 Francesca Martin

Printed in Hong Kong

British Library Cataloguing in Publication Data
A catalogue record for this book is
available from the British Library

ISBN 0-7445-3160-8

The Honey Hunters

A traditional African tale illustrated by

Francesca Martin

WALKER BOOKS
AND SUBSIDIARIES
LONDON • BOSTON • SYDNEY

Once upon a time all the wild animals were the greatest of friends. And, as it happened, they all loved honey. The little grey honey-guide knew the best places to find honey. "Che, che! Cheka, cheka, che!" the bird would cry. "If you want honey, follow me!"

One day a boy was walking by the lake
when he heard the honey-guide's song.
"I'd like some honey," he said. "I'll follow you."
And so the boy and the honey-guide set off
together through the forest.

Very soon they met a cock.

"Che, che! Cheka, cheka, che!" sang the
honey-guide. "If you want honey, follow me!"

"I'd like some honey," said the cock, fluffing up
his tail feathers. "I'll follow you."

And so the cock joined the boy as he followed
the honey-guide through the forest.

They had not gone far when
they saw a bush cat.

"Che, che! Cheka, cheka, che!" sang the
honey-guide. "If you want honey, follow me!"

"I'd like some honey," said the bush cat,
dropping from the tree. "I'll follow you."

So the honey-guide and the boy and the cock
and the bush cat set off together.

By and by they
met an antelope …

and then
a leopard …

and then
a zebra …

and then
a lion …

"Che, che! Cheka, cheka che!" the honey-guide sang to each of the animals. "If you want honey, follow me!" So the antelope and the leopard, the zebra and the lion, joined the boy and the cock and the bush cat as they followed the honey-guide through the forest.

Pretty soon the animals met an elephant.

"Where are you all going, my friends?" he asked.

"To find some honey," replied the boy.

"Che, che! Cheka, cheka, che!" sang the honey-guide.

"If you want honey, follow me!"

So the elephant joined the procession
of animals going in search of honey.

In a short while, the honey-guide stopped.

"Che, che! Cheka, cheka, che!" he sang again.

"If you want honey, look in this tree!"

Then the boy took a beautiful honeycomb

from the bees' nest and broke it into four pieces.

The first he gave to the cock and the bush cat.

The second he gave to the antelope and the leopard.

The third he gave to the zebra and the lion.

And the fourth he kept for himself and the elephant.

Then all the animals began to eat…

The cock pecked his end of the honeycomb and the bush cat licked his. Then the bush cat spat at the cock and the cock scratched the bush cat.

The antelope nibbled her end of the honeycomb and the leopard gulped his. Then the leopard clawed the antelope and the antelope kicked the leopard.

The zebra chewed her end
of the honeycomb and the
lion tore off a big chunk.
Then the lion leapt upon the
zebra and the zebra bit the
lion with her sharp teeth.

The elephant seized the last
honeycomb from the boy
and swallowed it whole.
And the boy simply stood
and stared in amazement
at the squabbling animals.

"Stop! Stop!" cried the boy in alarm. "Don't fight!
You have never quarrelled with each other before!"
But the animals refused to listen.
Then the boy grew very angry. He seized a
stick and threatened to beat every one of them.

At this, the animals fell silent.

Then the elephant spoke. "The damage is done," he said sadly. "We can never be friends again. From now on we shall be enemies: the cock and the bush cat, the antelope and the leopard, the zebra and the lion, and myself and man."

Then all the animals turned and disappeared into the bush.

Only the boy and the honey-guide remained.
"Che, che! Cheka, cheka, che!" sang the
honey-guide. "If you want honey, follow me."
Still singing his jaunty song, the little bird
flew off into the bush. And – after a
moment's pause – his friend followed.

MORE WALKER PAPERBACKS
For You to Enjoy

LOTTIE'S CATS
by Mirabel Cecil / Francesca Martin

Lottie is an only child but she is never lonely. For she has seven cats
to keep her company – one for every day of the week!

"Will win over many readers… Ravishing illustrations complement a sensitive,
pleasingly old-fashioned text." *Susan Hill, The Sunday Times*

0-7445-2340-0   £3.99

PETER AND THE WOLF
by Selina Hastings / Reg Cartwright

A lively retelling of Sergei Prokofiev's popular orchestral tale.

"Well told and richly illustrated." *The Good Book Guide*

0-7445-0990-4   £3.99

THE MOUSEHOLE CAT
by Antonia Barber / Nicola Bayley

This dramatic and moving Cornish tale of Mowzer, the cat, and Tom, the old fisherman,
who brave the fury of the Great Storm Cat, was the children's choice for the Smarties Book Prize
and winner of the British Book Award (Illustrated Children's Book of the Year).

"A glorious tale. Nicola Bayley has here brought off the triumph of a lifetime… A book to wallow in,
read and re-read, for any age from five or so to very grown-up." *The Sunday Times*

0-7445-2353-2   £4.99

Walker Paperbacks are available from most booksellers, or by post from B.B.C.S., P.O. Box 941, Hull, North Humberside HU1 3YQ
24 hour telephone credit card line 01482 224626
To order, send: Title, author, ISBN number and price for each book ordered, your full name and address,
cheque or postal order payable to BBCS for the total amount and allow the following for postage and packing:
UK and BFPO: £1.00 for the first book, and 50p for each additional book to a maximum of £3.50.
Overseas and Eire: £2.00 for the first book, £1.00 for the second and 50p for each additional book.
Prices and availability are subject to change without notice.